The FED-UP Cow

Peta Lemon   Maria Dasic Todoric

This book is dedicated to the cow I saw that day in a field, who looked fed-up, and who inspired me to write this story.

QUIRKY PICTURE PRESS

Hilda was FED-UP with being a cow.
She wanted a change and wanted it now.
Spending all day doing not much but moo.
There had to be something better to do.

She looked round the fields and spotted the sheep.
"Sheep do much more than milk, eat and sleep.
Sheep have such lovely curly white hair.
And get a haircut."

This wasn't fair!

Hilda did not like her brown spotty hide.
She wanted a look to show off with pride.
So Hilda did something you may think... strange.
From cow to a sheep she decided to change.

First, she needed sheep hair for her head.
So off to the wig shop she frantically fled.
And chose the one with the biggest white curls.
Then rushed back to show it off to the girls.

Her friends took one look and fell in a heap,
with side-splitting chortles.

A cow as a
sheep!

She said her goodbyes and climbed in with the rams.
And tried to lie down and cuddle the lambs.

But the sheep took
one look at Hilda
and fled.

Leaving her muddled
and scratching
her head.

Hilda's life as a sheep didn't go well.
Her wig got all knotted and started to smell.
Some birds thought her wig would make a good nest.
And lined up to use it for somewhere to rest.

On haircut day Hilda was first in the queue.

But the shearer saw her and told her to "Shooooooo!"

I cannot cut that big smelly lump.

That wig must be thrown away in the dump!"

Hilda got cross and puffed up her wig.

But then she spotted a pretty pink pig.

"Sheep don't do much more than chew grass and bleat.
The life of a pig you surely can't beat.
Pigs have those charming curly pink tails.
And eat all day long from those big metal pails."

Hilda did not like her curly white hair.
She wanted a look with a little more flair.
So Hilda did something you may think … strange.
From sheep to a pig she decided to change.

She slapped on some paint to make herself pink.

Rolled in manure so that she would stink.

The tail she made with an old piece of string.

Then she trotted around once she'd done everything.

She glanced at the
sheep and waved
them goodbye.

And joyfully
jumped in
the pig sty.

The pigs took one
look and laughed
till it hurt.

Then carried on
rolling around in
the dirt.

Hilda's life as a pig didn't go well.
She just couldn't bear the pongy pig smell.

Eating all day made her tummy get sore.

As soon as they'd finished, the pigs shouted "MORE!!"

The scoffing and snorting made Hilda get snappy.
And it wasn't long till she was unhappy.

"Pigs are so greedy and STINK of poop."

But then she spotted the chicken coop....

"A hen. Of course! That's what I should be.
Being a hen is perfect for me.

Their feathers are
simply sumptuous
to touch.

And sitting on eggs?
I want that
so much!"

Hilda did not like being all mucky.
She wanted to look more homely and clucky.
So Hilda did something you may think... strange.
From pig to a hen she decided to change.

She stuck on some feathers she found round her hooves.

And clucked around with
some chicken-like moves.

Then announced to the hens:

"I'm here at long last!"

And squeezed in the coop without being asked.

The hens got so cross. It was a disgrace
that this cow came along and took all their space.

Hilda's life as a hen didn't go well.
Her legs got all cramped and started to swell.

She waited.....

...... and waited for fresh eggs to come.....

But ended with nothing but a sore bum.

After a week Hilda groaned,
"This is bad, the pecking and clucking is driving me mad."

She peeled off her
feathers onto the floor.

"I just cannot be a hen anymore."

Then Hilda spotted
something....

AMAZING!

A herd of brown cows was happily grazing.
The afternoon sun shone down on their heads.
As they went to lie down on their homely hay beds.

"A cow….. A cow!
Why couldn't I see?
It's WONDERFUL to just be me."

"I am a beautiful brown spotty cow.
And I will join my friends again now."

From then Hilda's life was contented.

And FUN!

And she smiled when she
thought of the things
she had done.

97515861R00021